Donated in memory of

Wilton Hunter Talley &

Elizabeth Almond Talley

By Julia Talley Draucker

August, 1994

OLYMPIC GOLD!

CARL LEWIS

by
Wayne Coffey

BLACKBIRCH PRESS, INC.
Woodbridge, Connecticut

Published by Blackbirch Press, Inc.
One Bradley Road
Woodbridge, CT 06525

©1993 Blackbirch Press, Inc.
First Edition

All rights reserved. No part of this book may be reproduced in any form without permission in writing from Blackbirch Press, Inc. except by a reviewer.

Manufactured in the United States of America
10 9 8 7 6 5 4 3 2 1

Editor: Bruce Glassman
Photo Research: Grace How
Illustrations: David Taylor

Library of Congress Cataloging-in-Publication Data

Coffey, Wayne R.
   Carl Lewis / by Wayne Coffey. — 1st ed.
     p.   cm. — (Olympic gold!)
   Includes bibliographical references and index.
   Summary: A biography of the American athlete who won medals in several track and field events in the 1984, 1988, and 1992 Olympic games.
   ISBN 1-56711-006-1   ISBN 1-56711-052-5 (pbk.)
   1.Lewis, Carl, 1961-   —Juvenile Literature. 2. Athletes—United States—Biography—Juvenile literature. [1. Lewis, Carl, 1961- . 2. Track and field athletes. 3. Afro-Americans—Biography.] I. Title. II.Series.
GV697.L48C64 1993
796'.092—dc20
[B]   92-45545
                                                                           CIP
                                                                            AC

Photo Credits

Cover: ©N. Russell/Gamma-Liaison; cover detail: AP/Wide World Photos; back cover: ©David Kennerly/Gamma-Liaison; p.4: ©Francis Apesteguy/Gamma-Liaison; p. 33: ©Kennerly/Gamma-Liaison; pp. 34, 35, 36 (top), 40, 42–43: Focus On Sports; p.36 (bottom): ©Kennerly/Gamma-Liaison; p.38–39: Gamma-Liaison; p. 39 (top): AP/Wide World Photos; p.41 (top): Gamma-Liaison; pp. 37, 41 (bottom), 42 (top), 44, 45, 46, 47, 48: AP/Wide World Photos.

Contents

Chapter 1 **Sticking with It**   5

Chapter 2 **The Thrill of Winning**   13

Chapter 3 **The Dream Comes Alive**   20

Chapter 4 **Disappointment and Hope**   29

          A Picture Portfolio   33

Chapter 5 **On Top of the World**   54

          Glossary   63
          For Further Reading   63
          Index   64

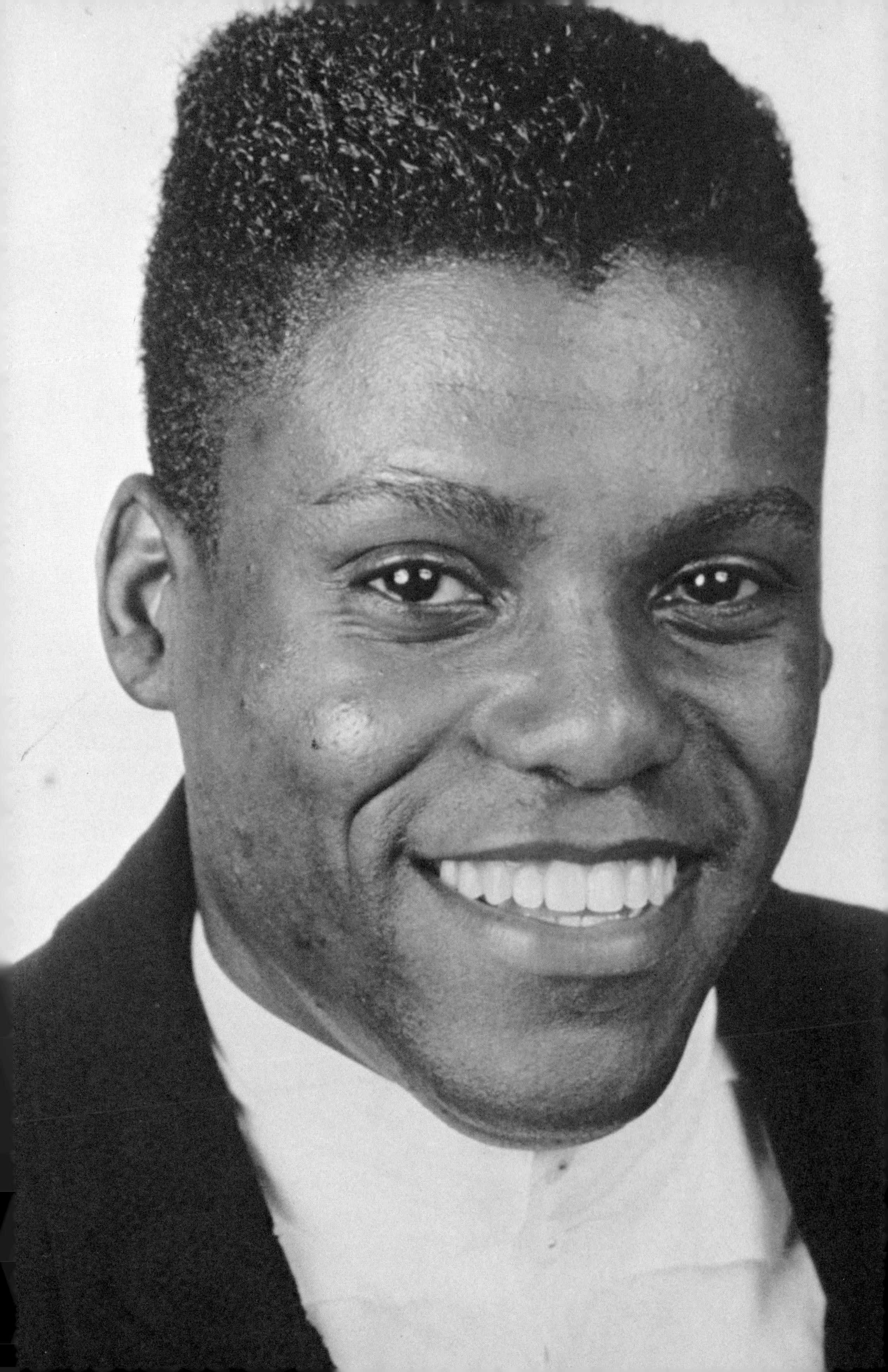

1

Sticking with It

"It's all a question of how much you want to win."

Years before Carl Lewis became one of the greatest athletes in track-and-field history, he learned a lot about losing. When he was young, Carl and his friends would hold races. Carl was a small, slight youngster then, and he would almost never win. After one discouraging setback, Carl told his father that he wasn't sure he wanted to race anymore. "I'm tired of losing all the time," Carl said.

Bill Lewis told his son that he had two choices. He could quit, or he could work to get better. "Only through continued effort will you be able to run faster and jump farther," Bill Lewis said. "It's all a question of how much you want to win."

Opposite:
Carl Lewis is widely regarded as one of the greatest track-and-field athletes of all time.

Olympic Gold!

Carl took his father's message to heart. In time, after much practice, he was outracing all his friends in the schoolyard. Years later, he was doing much better than that—he was outracing the whole world.

Today, the name *Carl Lewis* is stamped all over the Olympic record books. He has beaten many of the records set by Jesse Owens, his boyhood idol. Jesse Owens won four gold medals in the 1936 Summer Olympics in Berlin, Germany.

Carl Lewis has been a member of the U.S. Olympic squad four times. The first time was in 1980, when the Summer Olympics were held in Moscow, USSR. The U.S. team wound up staying home in protest because the Soviet Union had invaded neighboring Afghanistan.

A Gifted Family

Frederick Carlton Lewis was born on July 1, 1961, in Birmingham, Alabama—the same state that produced Jesse Owens. There was every reason to believe that Carl would grow into a superb athlete one day.

William and Evelyn Lewis, Carl's parents, were tremendously gifted in a variety of sports. Bill played football and ran track for Tuskegee Institute in Alabama, excelling in the long jump and the sprints. Evelyn played basketball at Tuskegee and also

From an early age, Carl idolized Jesse Owens, who had won four gold track-and-field medals in the 1936 Olympics.

became one of the top players in the nation. In 1951, she represented the United States in the Pan American Games. Evelyn had a terrific chance of making the U.S. Olympic team a year later until an injury forced her to the sidelines.

These athletic skills were passed on to all four Lewis children. Mack, Carl's oldest brother, was a high-school track stand-out who set county records. Cleve, another brother, was such an accomplished soccer player that he became the first American to

7

be drafted by the pros in that sport. Cleve went on to play for a team called the Memphis Rogues.

The only girl in the family, Carol, two years younger than Carl, may have been blessed with more ability than any of her brothers. She and Carl were constant playmates as children. Carol became a top-ranked long jumper and sprinter—the same combination that made Carl famous.

Competing with a Little Sister

Carl discovered at a young age how much he enjoyed athletics. His parents launched a track club in Willingboro, New Jersey, where the family moved when Carl was two years old.

Carl had interests other than sports, such as playing the cello and the drums. There were times when he wondered if he were better suited to music than sports. Sometimes his parents wondered, too. Young Carl was the runt of the family. Bill and Evelyn Lewis didn't want to hurt their son's feelings, but the boy simply didn't seem as gifted as the rest of the family.

Jesse Owens Takes Notice

Carl stuck to his goals, and it wasn't long before he started showing the same athletic skill that the other Lewises had. In nearby

Philadelphia, when Carl was 12, he won the long-jump event at a meet conducted by a group called the Jesse Owens Youth Program. The Olympic legend was on hand to watch, and he couldn't help but be impressed by the spindly Carl Lewis. "You should learn a lesson from this smaller guy," Jesse told the other competitors. "He was determined and he really tried hard." Carl also remembered something else Jesse Owens said: "Have fun. If you're not having fun playing a sport, what's the sense of playing?"

"You should learn a lesson from this smaller guy," Jesse Owens once said of the young Carl.

Though Carol was constantly bringing home trophies and certificates from all her victories, as Carl grew older, he started winning, too. "I didn't mature until high school, while others began maturing in seventh, eighth grade," Carl said. "The talent was there all the time, but it was only when I got older that I really blossomed."

Setting a High-School Record

Carl's body didn't grow as much as it "exploded." He sprouted so rapidly that at age 15, he had to use crutches for a short time as he adjusted to his new size and strength. When Carl entered his junior year at Willingboro High, many of his friends barely recognized him.

Olympic Gold!

Some track-and field-rivals had difficulty recognizing him, too. At the start of his junior year, his time in the 100-yard dash was 10.6 seconds. Not long after, he cut his time down to 9.8. At the end of that year, in the national junior championships in Memphis, Tennessee, he cut it down even lower—to 9.3, an astonishing improvement in just a few months.

Meanwhile, Carl's long jumping ability was attracting still more attention. Even as a scrawny freshman, he jumped 22 feet. Before long, he was jumping 23, 24, then 25 feet. At that same championship meet in Memphis, he set a national high-school

As a teenager, Carl's body grew so fast that he needed crutches to adjust to his new size and strength.

record with a leap of 25 feet 9 inches. In his senior year, in 1979, Carl increased his mark to 26 feet 8 inches. That was only one quarter of an inch shy of the world record Jesse Owens had set in 1935—a record that lasted for 25 years. And Carl was still just a 17-year-old high-school student.

The Dream Begins

The rapidly progressing athletic teenager had admired Jesse Owen's accomplishments for years. Carl dreamed of being an Olympic star and also of one day being like Bob Beamon.

Bob Beamon turned in what is widely regarded as the greatest performance in Olympic track-and-field history. It came on October 18, 1968, in the high altitude of Mexico City. On that day, Beamon soared through the air in what seemed a superhuman feat. When he landed, the officials bent down and made their measurements. They checked them several times because the reading was, well, unbelievable. The number was posted: 8.9 meters. That converted to 29 feet 2 1/2 inches—nearly 2 feet farther than the world record!

Beamon's momentous achievement made a big impression on a youngster in southern New Jersey. In his backyard, Carl Lewis measured the distance of Beamon's jump.

By the time Carl was a senior in high school, he had already jumped 26 feet 8 inches—just a quarter inch short of the world record set by Jesse Owens.

He gazed at the end of the tape, amazed that a person could jump so far.

Fifteen years after Bob Beamon's jump, Carl wrapped up a record-setting career at Willingboro High. Sorting through dozens of scholarship offers, he enrolled at the University of Houston, which was coached by Tom Tellez, a widely respected expert in track and field. Carl Lewis's chase of the Olympic legends, Jesse Owens and Bob Beamon, was about to begin in earnest.

2

The Thrill of Winning

"Jesse Owens was such a big figure in my life....To be put in the same category is to flatter me."

As excited as he was to coach such a splendid athlete as Carl Lewis, Tom Tellez had concerns almost immediately. Carl's long jumping style, which propelled him high into the air, placed tremendous stress on his legs. His takeoffs were so jarring that he once shredded two metal spikes right off the bottom of his track shoe. His knees frequently became swollen and tender. Carl's athletic career was still in its early stages, but his knees surely could not take such a pounding for long.

A Demanding Coach

Coach Tellez wanted Carl to make major changes in his approach. The coach was not only demanding, but he was very good at explaining the reasoning behind his advice. It was Tellez's technical command of the sport that had influenced Carl to go to the University of Houston. The more the coach talked, the more his suggestions made sense to Carl.

Tellez clocked Carl at 27 miles per hour as he sped down the runway toward the board. The coach taught his new pupil how he could take full advantage of that sprinter's speed by improving his thrust forward rather than trying to jump so high. While Carl was in the air, Tellez instructed him to use a method called the "hitch kick," a pedaling motion of the arms and legs that could squeeze extra distance out of a jump. The idea with a long jump is to have maximum "horizontal velocity," Tellez had always believed. After all, the goal isn't height, but distance.

Only a rare athlete could succeed at this unique method of jumping, which requires a remarkable sense of balance as the performer is high-kicking in the air. It also takes great precision. All the elements have to be carefully timed and executed.

It wasn't easy for Carl at first. Years of doing things the old way had to be erased. Despite this, it didn't take Carl long to improve his distance under Tellez.

Amazing Progress

Carl made the U.S. Olympic team when he was just 18 years old. Less than a year later, in the National Collegiate Athletic Association (NCAA) outdoor championships in Baton Rouge, Louisiana, he placed first in the 100-yard dash with a time of 9.99 seconds, which was aided by a tail wind. This was just four one-hundredths of a second shy of the world record, held by Jim Hines. Carl also won the long jump with a leap of 27 feet 3/4 inch. It marked the first time since 1936 that an athlete had won in both a track and a field event in the same NCAA outdoor championships. The last man to do it? Jesse Owens.

Carl Lewis was mobbed by reporters afterward, answering a constant stream of questions about his achievement. "It's the biggest thrill of my life," Carl told them. "Jesse Owens was such a big figure in my life, as well as in track and field. A person like him will live on forever. To put me in the same category is to flatter me. He's an inspiration."

Even Tellez was astounded by his young pupil's progress. "When you get an athlete like Carl, well, that's what you dream about," the coach said. "He has a great physical sense of what he's supposed to do. Once he gets that going, then it all unfolds.

Olympic Gold!

Carl's coach at the University of Houston taught Carl to use a "hitch kick" technique while jumping in order to increase his distance.

Everything he's done has not been by accident. It has been planned." Carl Lewis, the coach once said, "is a physical genius."

After the NCAA wins, Carl Lewis's career took off the way Lewis did himself, over the sandpit. At the U.S. outdoor track-and-field championships in Sacramento, California, Carl won the 100-yard dash in 10.13 seconds. In the long jump, Carl leaped 28 feet 3 1/2 inches. It was the second longest jump in track-and-field history, behind Bob Beamon. To conserve his energy for the 100-yard dash, Carl passed on his next five attempts. His main rival, the man then considered the top jumper in the country, was Larry Myricks. Larry had defeated Carl in eight of their nine long-jump duels prior to that. On his fifth jump, Larry produced his best effort of the day, a jump of 27 feet 8 3/4 inches. As superb a jump as it was, it wasn't even a half-foot within Carl Lewis's jump. Nobody knew it then, but Carl was starting a long-jump winning streak that would span 65 meets and 10 years. Larry Myricks had outjumped Carl in February of 1981. The next time anyone would be able to make that claim would be in August of 1991.

"Carl Lewis," Coach Tellez once said, "is a physical genius."

Proving Others Wrong

There were plenty of track-and-field people, both competitors and officials, who were certain that Carl would someday pay a price for putting his body through the strain of jumping and sprinting at the same meets.

After one race in which Carl suffered a slight muscle pull and finished last, a rival said to him, "See, I told you, you can't do the one hundred and the jump in the same day. It takes too much out of you." But the more people doubted him, the more determined Carl was to prove them wrong.

A Controversial Jump

Carl was quickly becoming one of the biggest track-and-field attractions in the world. He was a performer who could set a record nearly every time out. In 1981, he was given the Sullivan Award for being the most outstanding amateur athlete in the country. A year later, at the National Sports Festival in Indianapolis, he continued to close in on Bob Beamon, with a winning jump of 28 feet 9 inches. What stirred even more excitement, however, was a jump that is nowhere in the record books. Should it be? Many people think so.

On the controversial jump, Carl streaked down the runway and appeared to have a good takeoff. He flew through the air, all the way toward the back of the pit. It was a remarkable leap. As a charge surged through the crowd, Carl sensed it was the greatest jump of his life. Suddenly, the thrill drained out of him. An official held up a flag, ruling a foul. (A claylike substance is sprinkled beyond the takeoff board so judges can determine if a jumper has fouled. The substance showed no signs of being disturbed.) The jump, to many observers, looked perfectly legal. But the official would not budge. By most accounts, that jump was close to 30 feet.

Triple Gold at Helsinki

In 1983, the first world championships of track and field were held in Helsinki, Finland. Carl Lewis won three gold medals by taking the 100-meter dash and the long jump and running the last leg of a world-record 400-meter relay. The next week, the cover of *Sports Illustrated* magazine had a picture of Carl Lewis, along with the words: "The Best in the World . . . Carl Lewis scores a stunning triple in Helsinki."

Facing the Olympic Challenge

Carl Lewis's accomplishments were piling up as fast as all the headlines. The next challenge he faced was the greatest one yet—the 1984 Olympics in Los Angeles, the first time the Summer Games had been held in the United States in more than 50 years. The entire country would be glued to the event. It almost seemed as if nobody in the world had higher expectations placed on him than Carl Lewis.

3

The Dream Comes Alive
"I had the time of my life."

If there was any downside to Carl Lewis's rise to fame, it was that he never really felt comfortable in the spotlight. As a youngster, he was shy and quiet, and he preferred to stay to himself. Now, all of a sudden, his every action, and every statement, was big news for the media all over the world.

The press conferences never seemed to end. Neither did the questions. Carl tried to be pleasant and polite, because he understood that reporters had a job to do. His business agent, Joe Douglas, also told him that all the publicity could mean a great deal more money for Carl. But dealing with the media still wasn't easy.

Public Criticism

Carl became even less comfortable after negative stories began to appear. Most of them made Carl seem selfish and cold, a man whose main goal was to promote himself. Several competitors made stinging criticisms of him that were read by millions in scores of newspapers. At the national championships in 1983, Carl won gold medals in the 100- and 200-meter races and the long jump, becoming the first athlete to do so in almost 100 years. Near the end of the 200-meter race, when he knew victory was secure, he threw his arms over his head in early celebration. Carl wound up with an American record time of 19.75 seconds but missed the world record, quite possibly because he raised his arms before he finished.

Around 1983, Carl became the subject of stories in the press. Some competitors felt Carl was too arrogant and sure of himself.

"There is going to be some serious celebrating when Carl gets beat," said an angry Larry Myricks, who finished second that day. Edwin Moses, a record-breaking hurdler, suggested that Carl could try to be more humble.

Carl insisted that he meant no harm to anyone. He simply was so overjoyed about his historic triple victory that he displayed his emotions, without thinking about it. If people took that the wrong way, Carl felt that was their problem. In any case, he understood that a number of top American athletes, people such as Ted Williams, Kareem Abdul-Jabbar, and Muhammad Ali, had also been widely criticized over the years. He had plenty of company.

Whatever people wanted to say or write about him, there was no arguing that Carl had a great ability to concentrate and compete. And the bigger the meet, the greater his concentration. As he prepared for his first Olympics, in Los Angeles, he wasn't going to let anything interfere with his performance.

Winning the Olympic Trials

The first test for Carl was the 100 meters, which was considered the event in which he would have the toughest time winning. Actually, it was an accomplishment just to qualify for the U.S. team. In the Olympic trials, Carl's rivals included Calvin Smith, who had recently set a world record, and Mel Lattany, whose fastest running record of 9.96 seconds was better than any of Carl's records. There were also many other world-class sprinters, but competition had always brought out the best in Carl. This time was no different. Carl won the trials and was determined to repeat his victory in the Games themselves.

The First Gold Medal

When the gun sounded for the 100-meter finals, Sam Graddy, Carl's U.S. teammate, powered out of the starter's blocks to take the early lead. Ron Brown, another fellow American who later played in the National Football League, was also a threat. (He had beaten Carl in a meet a few months earlier.) Carl was behind in the race immediately, but that didn't concern him much. At six feet two inches, Carl is unusually tall for a sprinter. The extra inches make it slightly harder for him to come out of his starting crouch. His trademark as a sprinter has always been maintaining his blinding speed late in the race, when his rivals are slowing down.

"The reason I'm so powerful in the late forty or fifty meters," he explained, "is because I can relax very well, and when you relax, you don't lose as much speed. Everybody loses speed from about sixty meters to the finish line—everybody. But the one who loses the least has the strongest finish."

Carl was competing against many world-class sprinters, but competition had always brought out the best in him.

True to his history, Carl stayed relaxed as he raced down the coliseum straightaway. Halfway through the race, he was in third place, and many fans figured he was in deep trouble. But in the next few seconds,

Olympic Gold!

Sam Graddy began to fade, and Carl was suddenly catching up in a hurry. At the 80-meter mark, Carl streaked into the lead. By 90 meters, he was well ahead. By the time he crossed the coliseum finish line, Carl had a time of 9.99 seconds—the widest margin of victory in the 100-meter dash in all of Olympic history. The massive crowd let out a deafening roar. Carl Lewis had his first gold medal.

A Second Gold Medal for Carl

When it came to the long jump, Carl was a big favorite. Only one other jumper in the field, Larry Myricks, had surpassed 28 feet. It was a cool, windy Monday night in Los Angeles. Carl's first jump was 28 feet 1/2 inch—a fine effort, given the difficult conditions. On his second jump, his timing was off. When he hit the board, he just kept running, right into the pit.

A long jumper has the right to pass on his turn if he chooses to do so. Carl wound up passing on all of his remaining four chances. Nobody was threatening him, and he was suffering from a sore hamstring. With the enormous strain required for each jump, he thought the rest was more important. After all, he still had two more events.

Carl's jump won him his second gold medal, but he found himself in the middle of a controversy once again. Some fans in the coliseum booed him when he declined to take any more jumps. They were hoping to see Carl break Bob Beamon's record and they felt cheated that he wasn't even going to try. One reporter, sympathizing with the fans, compared it with going to a Frank Sinatra concert and having him sing just one song.

More Olympic Gold!
During his medal ceremony, Carl was cheered by many of the fans, but it was still hard for him to swallow getting booed. With the cool temperature and swirling

Fans who were disappointed with Carl's passes in the 1984 long-jump competition booed him during the medal ceremony.

25

Olympic Gold!

wind, there was no way he was going to threaten Beamon that night. And it would have been foolish to risk further jumps with a tender leg. Carl remained convinced that he had done the right thing.

Boos aside, Carl was off to a sensational start—and he only got better. He won the 200-meter dash with the second fastest clocking of his career (19.80 seconds), setting an Olympic record in the process. Now the final test was the four man 100-meter relay (4 x 100-meter relay), in which

Carl and his teammates—Sam Graddy, Ron Brown, and Calvin Smith—would each run a 100-meter leg. Carl, however, would run the all-important last leg.

The American team was regarded as the best in the world, and the four runners lived up to the billing. When Carl crossed the finish line, the Olympic clock showed 37.83 seconds. They had set a world record! It was the only world mark that was broken in the Olympics that year. It seemed a perfect way for Carl Lewis to finish the

When Carl crossed the finish line after running the last leg of the 4 x 100-meter relay, the clock showed a new world record. In celebration, Carl carried an American flag in a victory lap around the track.

Games. Among the thousands of athletes who competed, he was by far the star. Not only had he duplicated the four gold medals that Jesse Owens had won in Berlin in 1936, he had lived up to all the expectations. Carl had been training for this event for years. He had dreamed of winning a gold medal even longer. And now it had happened, four times over.

An Unforgettable Experience

As he trotted around the track on his victory lap, Carl was handed a big American flag by a man in the stands, and he continued going around holding the flag. The next day, several people accused Carl of planting the man with the flag just to make himself look good. Carl said that was ridiculous. He said he had never seen the man before in his life.

When the 1984 Olympics began, the runner who had carried the Olympic torch into the stadium during the ceremonies was a young woman named Gina Hemphill. She was Jesse Owens's granddaughter. Gina was selected to honor the memory of Jesse's achievements. After the torch was lit, Carl Lewis honored Jesse Owens in his own way. He would never forget his first Olympic Games. He had made history. "I had the time of my life," Carl said.

4

Disappointment and Hope
"I'm going to get another one."

The bronze medalist in the 100-meter dash in Los Angeles was an explosive, Canadian named Ben Johnson. His time was 10.22 seconds, and though he was well behind Carl Lewis, his performance caught people by surprise.

Over the next few years, Ben Johnson emerged as the new sensation of track and field. After losing seven races in a row to Carl, Ben outran the Olympic champion in a meet in 1985. A year later, it was clear that "King Carl," as someone had nicknamed Lewis, wasn't the king of the sprints any longer. The Canadian's most brilliant effort came in Rome, Italy, during the 1987 world

Olympic Gold!

championships. After the Olympic Games, this was the most important track meet in the sports world. Ben set a world record with a time of 9.83 seconds—a full tenth of a second better than the former record, which was Carl Lewis's.

As the 1988 Summer Games approached, millions of fans around the world eagerly awaited the showdown between Ben and Carl. Although Ben owned the world record, he had suffered a few nagging injuries earlier in the year. Carl had beaten him in a meet in Switzerland just five weeks before the Games were to begin, in Seoul, South Korea. Carl was the defending Olympic champion. He wasn't going to give up the title easily.

Foul Play

The rivalry between the two sprinters went beyond the track. In recent months, Ben's personality had changed quite drastically. When he was a young competitor on the rise, Ben had been quiet and shy. Now he was a braggart. He talked about how awesome he was. In interviews he said that Carl could never beat him, that nobody could. And when Ben was in his best form, it seemed that he was right. His arms and legs were always powerful, but by now they were so huge that they looked as they might pop right out of his skin. Ben also had what everybody believed was the greatest start of any sprinter in history.

All these changes left Carl convinced that Ben was cheating by using steroids. The drugs not only make muscles much bigger, but they often make people moody and unpredictable. Steroid users also typically have a yellow tint in their eyes. Carl saw that in Ben, too. In an effort to stop drug use, Olympic officials gave athletes drug tests. But the tests don't always catch the cheaters, because there are other substances that can be taken that help to hide the presence of steroids.

Carl and Ben Johnson were long-time rivals who had a dramatic showdown in the 1988 Olympic 100-meter race.

Olympic Gold!

It really angered Carl that his rival was getting away with foul play. But what could Carl do? If he said anything, people would probably think he was jealous because somebody had come along and started beating him. Carl made a few remarks about the wide use of drugs in the sport, but other than that, he kept his mouth shut. He had had enough controversy in the 1984 Games and didn't want to distract himself with worrying about the personal problems of other athletes. All he wanted was to focus on running the best race he could.

It really angered Carl that his rival was getting away with foul play. But what could he do?

Competition Between Rivals

By the time September 24, 1988 arrived, the 100-meter showdown between Carl Lewis and Ben Johnson had become one of the most talked about events in all of Olympic history. A race that would take under 10 seconds to run had been analyzed for months and months. The semifinals were held just 90 minutes before the finals. Carl won his heat (qualifying race) and Ben won his, despite being furious after being called for a false start (a foul that is called when a runner leaves the blocks too early).

The moment the gun sounded in the Olympic final, Ben exploded forward. It

(Continued on page 49)

1984

LOS ANGELES, UNITED STATES

Early Victories

During the 1984 Games in Los Angeles, Carl Lewis burst onto the Olympic scene with a number of truly dazzling performances. He won his first gold medal in the 100-meter dash, setting a new Olympic record of 9.99 seconds. Carl's victory was won by the widest margin in Olympic history. His second gold medal came for his performance in the long jump, where he easily surpassed the other competitors with his first jump of 28 feet 1/4 inch. Carl then won his third gold medal in the 200-meter dash with an Olympic record-breaking time of 19.8 seconds—the second fastest time of his career. *Above*: Carl jumps to victory in the long jump. *Right*: Carl raises his arms in triumph as he crosses the finish line in record time for the 200-meter dash.

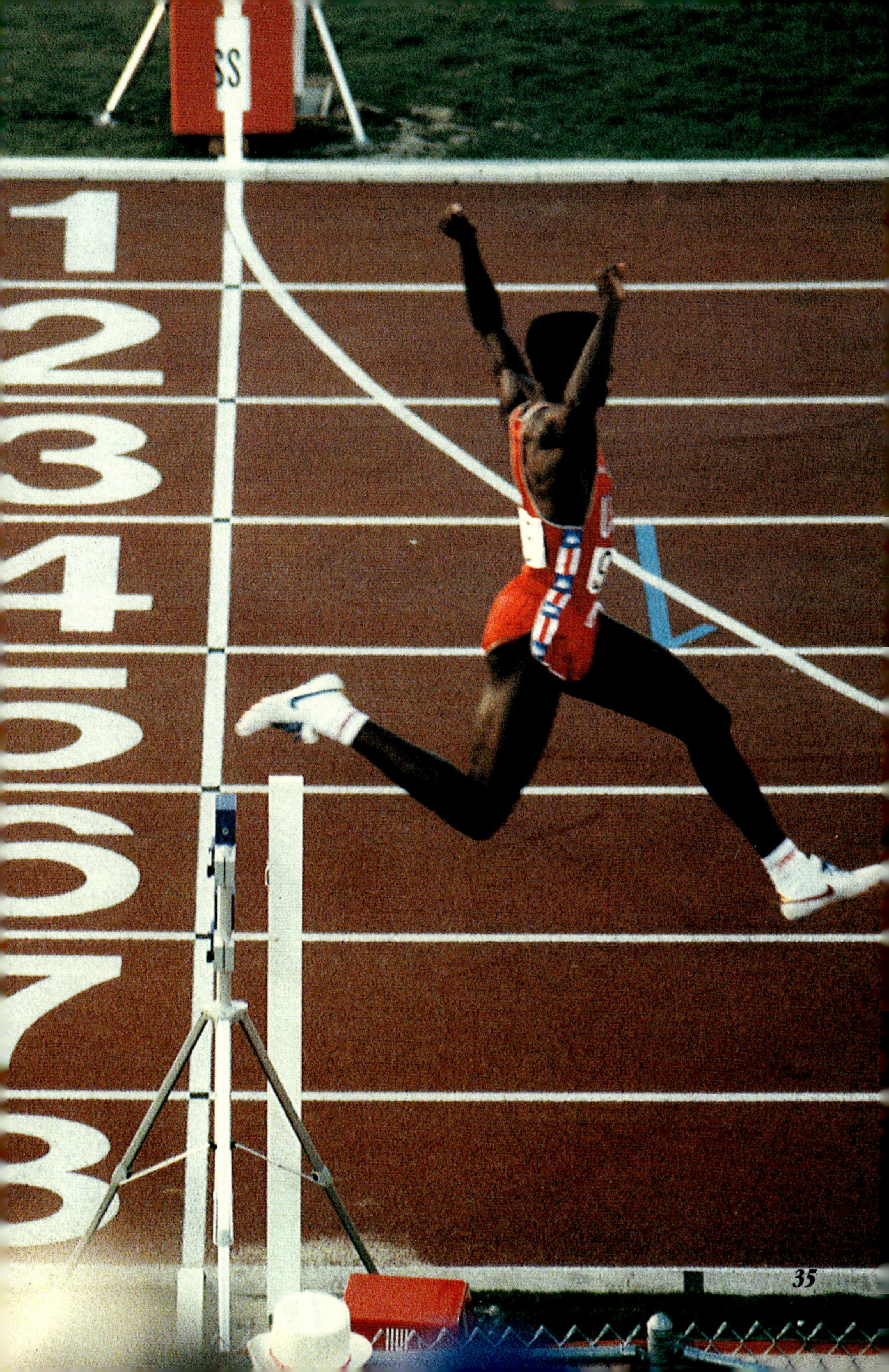

The Fourth Medal in '84

After winning three individual gold medals at the Los Angeles Games, Carl was faced with his final challenge: the four-man, 100-meter relay (4 x 100-meter relay). Carl was slotted to run the final 100-meter leg of the race for his teammates, Sam Graddy, Ron Brown, and Calvin Smith, who were already considered the best in the world. By the time Carl crossed the finish line, he had not only secured the gold medal for his team, he had also helped them to break a world record. The final time on the clock was 37.83 seconds, the only world record to be broken at the 1984 Games. *Above*: Carl bursts forward during the final leg of the record-breaking 4 x 100-meter relay. *Right*: The other three members of the U.S. relay team hoist Carl upon their shoulders as they celebrate their gold-medal performance.

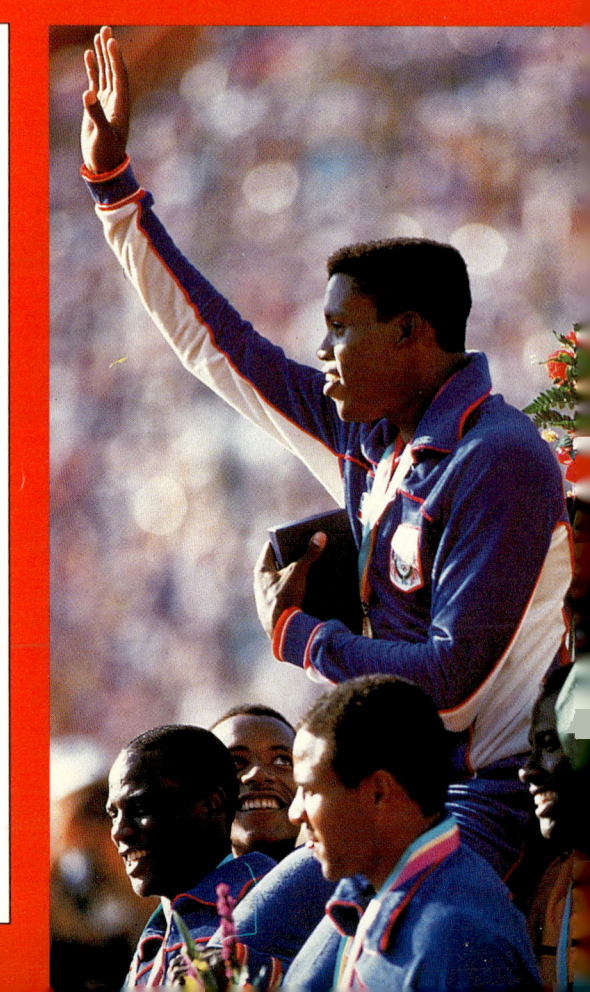

1988

Seoul, South Korea

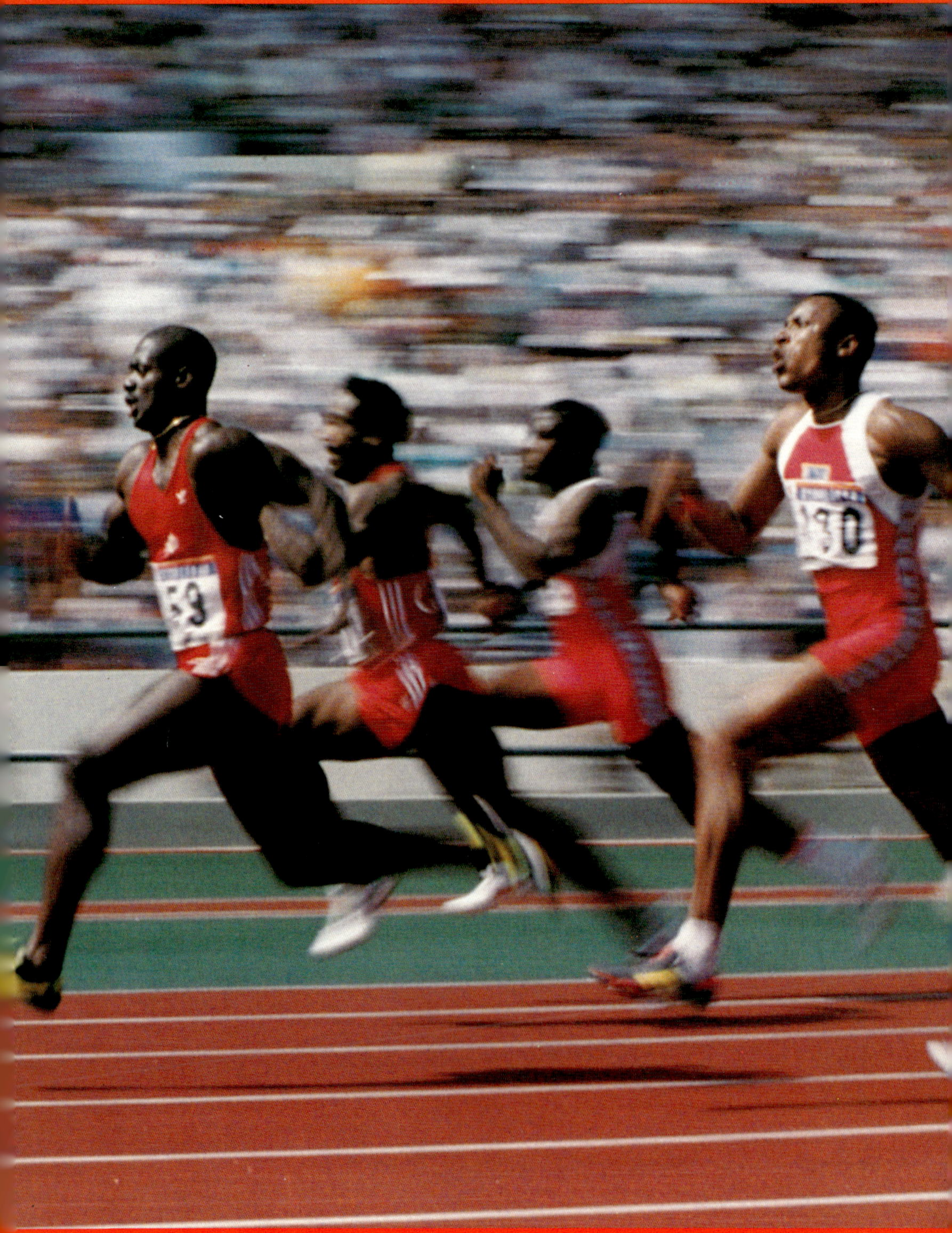

AN OLYMPIC CHALLENGE

By the time the 1988 Games in Seoul arrived, the world eagerly awaited a great 100-meter showdown between Carl Lewis and the new king of sprinting, Canadian Ben Johnson. The Canadian, who had beaten Carl the year before by setting a new world record at the world championships in Rome, Italy, seemed unstoppable. *Left:* When the gun sounded for the 100-meter contest, both Ben and Carl got off to a great start. At the 80-meter mark, Carl trailed Johnson by only five feet but, in the end, could not pull ahead. Johnson won the race with a world-record time of 9.79 seconds, a full .13 of a second faster than Carl. *Above:* Disappointed and upset, Carl could only look on as Johnson raised his finger in victory for the cheering crowd.

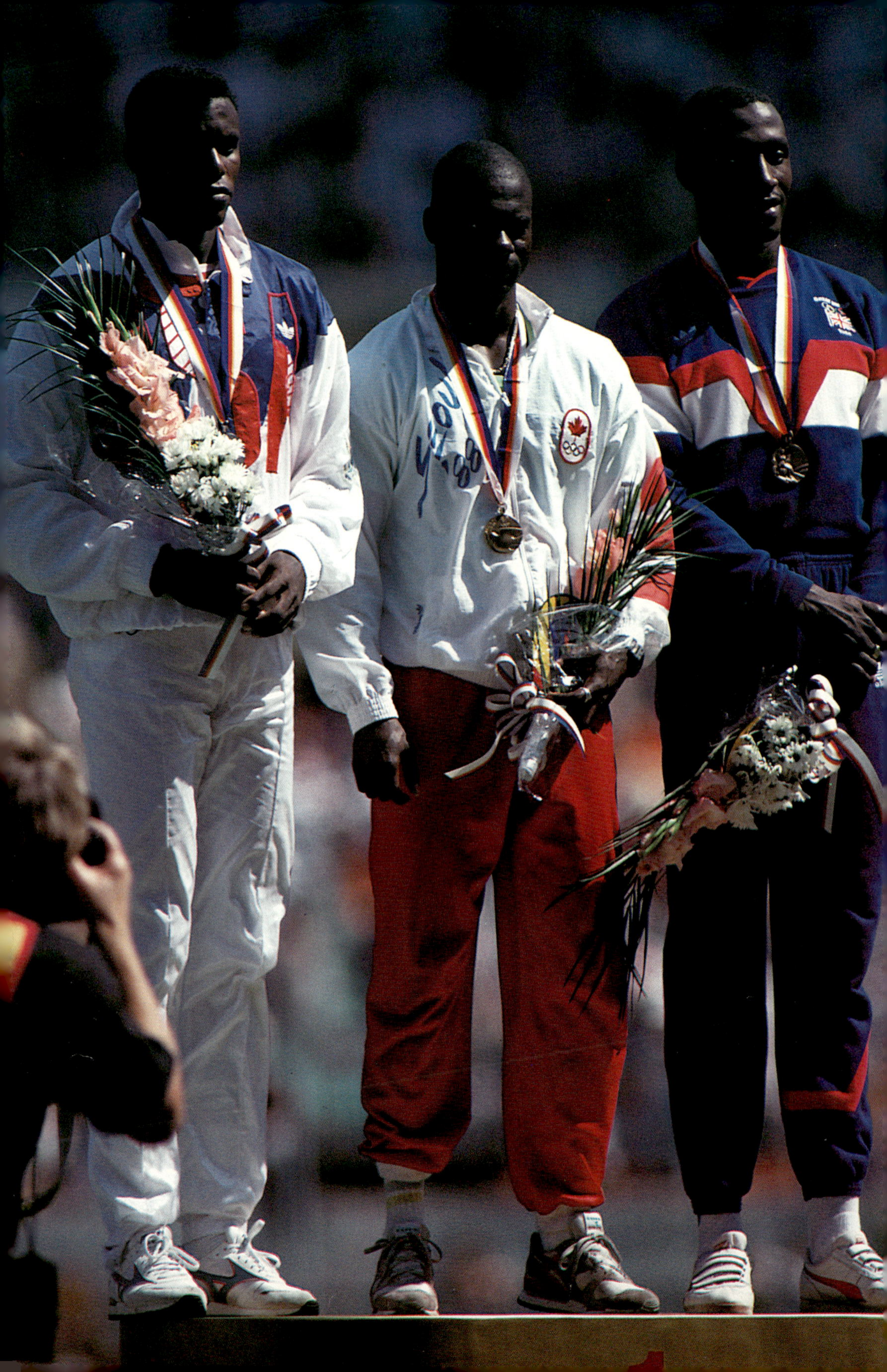

Accepting Second Place

Left: Ben Johnson (*center*) listens to the cheering crowd as he accepts the gold medal for the 100-meter race in 1988. Carl (*left*) stands with the silver medal around his neck, and Linford Christie (*right*) of Great Britain stands with his bronze medal. After his loss to Ben Johnson, Carl focused his Olympic energies on his remaining events. He went on to score the four best long jumps in the Games and led an American sweep of the event by winning his second consecutive long-jump gold medal (the first person in history to do that).
Right: Carl soars through the air in the long-jump competition.
Below: Carl waves to the crowd after making Olympic long-jump history.

A Triumph for Truth

Shortly after Carl's victory in the long jump, rumors began to circulate throughout Seoul that one of the athletes had tested positive for drug use. It was soon announced that the athlete was Canadian Ben Johnson, who had been illegally using steroids to build up his body. Johnson was immediately stripped of his medal and his record. The medal was then awarded to Carl in an official ceremony on October 1. *Above*: The rightful owner of the 1988 gold medal for the 100-meter dash proudly displays it for reporters.

Carl speeds past a Japanese runner to win a silver medal in the 200-meter race. Carl was edged out of the 200-meter gold medal by his teammate and close friend Joe DeLoach, who ran an Olympic-record time of 19.75 seconds. DeLoach was the first man in two years to beat Carl in that event.

CHAMPIONS IN TOKYO

After failing to qualify for the Olympic Games in Seoul, the U.S. relay team set out to reclaim their rightful place at the top of the relay world. In 1991, at the world championships in Tokyo, Japan, the relay team set a new world record of 37.50 seconds and went on to Barcelona, Spain, ready to defend their title. *Below:* Star anchorman Carl Lewis takes off after receiving the baton from teammate Dennis Mitchell in the 4 x 100-meter relay. *Right*: The American relay team revels in the glory of victory after winning the 1991 world championship. From left are Andre Cason, Carl Lewis, Leroy Burrell, and Dennis Mitchell.

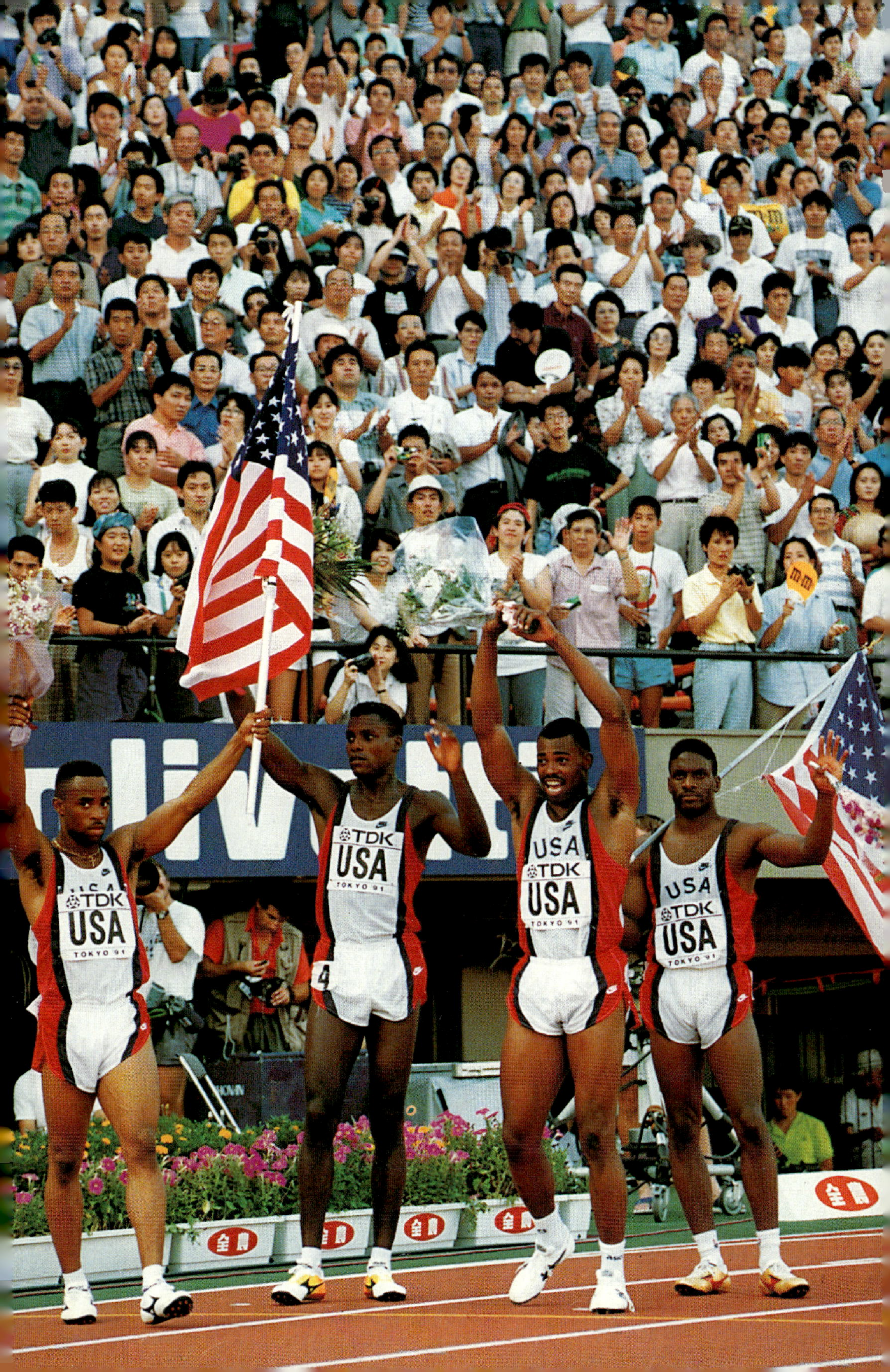
TDK
USA
TOKYO '91
全農

FASTEST MAN ALIVE
Carl carries an American flag around the track after his stunning victory in the 100-meter dash at the Tokyo world championships. Carl set a new world record by running the race in 9.86 seconds.

1992
BARCELONA, SPAIN

A Dazzling Finale

At the 1992 Games in Barcelona, Spain, Carl made Olympic history once again. After losing the world long-jump record to American teammate Mike Powell in Tokyo, Carl was determined to take back his title. The competition came down to a showdown between Carl and Powell; however, when the final measurements were taken, Carl had won the gold with a jump of 28 feet 5 1/2 inches. Not only had he won the gold, but he had also become the first person in history to win the long jump in three consecutive Olympics. Then, luck smiled on Carl again. After not qualifying for the relay team during the trials, Carl was asked to run in the finals when American teammate Mark Witherspoon suffered an injury. It turned out to be one of the greatest relays Carl had ever run. When he crossed the finish line, the Olympic scoreboard showed 37.40 seconds, a new world record. Carl had run his final 100 meters in 8.8 seconds, the fastest anyone had ever run.
Right: Carl flies through the air for a gold medal during the Barcelona long-jump competition.

(Continued from page 32)
was the best start of his life. Carl, famous for catching his rivals at the end of the race, had a good start, too. At the midway point, Ben Johnson had built a lead of about five feet, but Carl remained calm. He told himself, "I know I will catch him." Ben kept up his blazing pace. At the 80-meter mark, Ben still had the same lead. Carl kept charging, but it wasn't going to be enough. Ben Johnson was awesome. His time was another world record: 9.79 seconds. Carl ran a 9.92, the best time of his life, and still, he lost by a considerable margin.

Tens of thousands in the jam-packed stadium stood and cheered Ben Johnson. Back home in Canada, celebrations began instantly, reaching from the Atlantic to the Pacific. Ben was the first Canadian to capture a track-and-field gold medal since 1983. One newspaper headline summed up the delight. It read: BEN JOHNSON—A NATIONAL TREASURE.

Gracefully Accepting Defeat
As Ben flashed toward the tape, he stuck his arm over his head and raised one finger, then looked over toward Carl, just to make sure he knew who the number one man in the world was. Carl ignored this. He was burning inside, more certain than ever that his gold medal had been stolen by a

cheater. He shook Ben Johnson's hand and thought about how his father had always told him to behave with dignity and class whether you win or lose. Carl's dad had died in May of 1987, but his words lived on in Carl's memory.

Carl Sets a New Olympic Record

As disheartened as he was, Carl had three other events to prepare for. Two days later, in the most difficult day of his whole career, Carl had to run two qualifying races for the 200-meter dash, then compete in the long-jump finals. The sprints went well but took a lot out of him. He wasn't feeling very energetic as the final jumping started.

As he shook Ben Johnson's hand, Carl remembered that his father always told him to behave with dignity whether you win or lose.

On his first leap, Carl went 27 feet 7 inches. On the next one, he extended that to 28 feet. A few rounds later, Carl sprinted down the runway, hit the board just right, and registered a mark of 28 feet 7 1/4 inches. You sure couldn't tell he was tired! Carl had the best four jumps of the competition, as he led an American sweep of the event. Teammates Mike Powell and Larry Myricks captured the silver and bronze medals and Carl Lewis became the first man in Olympic history to win back-to-back long-jump titles.

A Victory for the Truth

Carl was still enjoying his triumphs when rumors started spreading all over Seoul. The word was that somebody had tested positive for drugs. A reporter called Carl at 3:30 A.M. to tell him. At first, details were very sketchy. Then more facts came out. The guilty athlete was believed to be a male sprinter. By later that morning, all the facts were in. The man who had tested positive for steroids was Canada's Ben Johnson. Ben denied the charges and insisted that the drug test had been fouled up. One of Johnson's advisors even suggested that somebody close to Carl might have switched the urine samples. Olympic officials did not buy this explanation. They stripped Ben Johnson of his gold medal and his world record. The new winner of the 100-meter dash was Carl Lewis.

The shocking story was on front pages all over the world. Ben Johnson had gone from a national treasure to a national disgrace. Much later, Ben admitted that he had lied when he made his denial. He told investigators he had been using steroids for years. Carl Lewis had every reason to delight in Ben's disgrace. But even though he knew that Ben had gotten what was coming to him, he didn't want to make the scandal worse. When asked about it,

Carl said, "I feel sorry for Ben and for the Canadian people. Ben is a great competitor, and I hope he is able to straighten out his life and return to competition."

Edged Out by a Friend

Carl's Olympic gold-medal total was now up to six. It didn't get any higher at Seoul, in part because Carl was such a good teacher. In the 200-meter final, Carl was nosed out for the gold by his young training partner and close friend, Joe DeLoach. Carl had the lead with just 50 meters to go, but the 21-year-old from Bay City, Texas, caught him as they sprinted toward the finish line. Joe ran an Olympic-record time of 19.75 seconds. He was the first man to beat Carl in the 200 meters in two years. Most athletes would be thrilled to win a medal of any sort in the Olympics, but winning silver after all those golds was difficult for Carl.

A Tough Break for the Americans

There was another disappointment, too, when the U.S. sprint-relay team failed to qualify for the Olympic finals. The Americans were the finest sprinters in the world, but a bad baton handoff between two of the runners resulted in a disqualification. Carl wasn't even competing that day. He was resting up for the finals. He wasn't surprised about the result, because a series of disagreements between runners and coaches on the team had created distractions and hard feelings.

This surely wasn't how Carl wanted the Olympics to end, but as he headed for home, he felt a deep sense of satisfaction just the same. His goal as a competitor had always been to give the best performances he was capable of, and he had done that.

Remembering His Father

The gold medal Carl won for the 100-meter dash was the most special of all, because it was in memory of his father. Bill Lewis was a loving, devoted father, a man who taught his son much about life. At his dad's funeral in May of 1987, as a way of expressing his thanks, Carl pulled out the gold medal from the 100-meter dash at the 1984 Olympics. He slipped the medal into his father's hands and said, "I want you to have this because it was your favorite event."

The gold medal Carl won for the 100-meter dash was the most special of all, because it was in memory of his father.

Carl's mother asked her son if he was sure he wanted the medal to be buried with his father. Carl said yes. He had also made a promise to his father as he handed him the medal. "I'm going to get another one," Carl said. At Seoul, he finally kept his promise.

5

On Top of the World

"No doubt about it. He's the best track-and-field athlete ever."

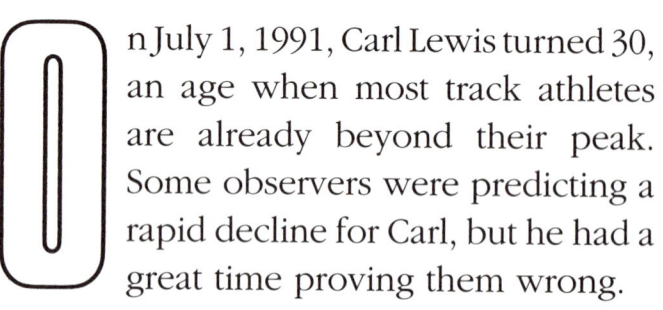

On July 1, 1991, Carl Lewis turned 30, an age when most track athletes are already beyond their peak. Some observers were predicting a rapid decline for Carl, but he had a great time proving them wrong.

Seven years after winning those memorable four gold medals in Los Angeles, Carl was actually running and jumping better than ever. In the 1991 national championships, held in New York City, he edged out Mike Powell to win the long jump, with a distance of 28 feet 4 1/4 inches. It was Carl's 65th long-jump victory in a row. To keep the astonishing winning streak intact, he had to come from behind, recording the winning jump on his sixth and final try of the competition.

At the same meet, Carl ran the 100-meter dash in 9.93 seconds, just a fraction off his best time ever. It would have been his best time, except for a sluggish start. The race was won by 24-year-old Leroy Burrell, who set a world record with a clocking of 9.90 seconds. Like Joe DeLoach in the 1988 Olympics, Leroy was a good friend and training partner of Carl's.

Better Than His Personal Best

A few months later, the world championships were held in Tokyo, Japan. Although Ben Johnson had returned to the sport after obeying a two-year ban, he was no longer much of a factor in the biggest races. Now the eyes of the world focused on Carl and his friend Leroy, the two fastest runners in history.

From the sound of the gun, every sprinter in the race was in peak form. Dennis Mitchell, another American, broke into the early lead. Leroy was close behind. At 60 meters, Carl was in about fifth place, but closing fast. He kept closing at 70 meters, and at 80 he was clearly in a different gear from everybody else. Leroy later said that Carl made everybody look as if they were standing still. Carl streaked through the tape, and when he looked at the stadium scoreboard, it was an unbelievable sight. He had run the greatest 100-meter race in history, clocking in at 9.86 seconds. Just as remarkable, Leroy ran a 9.88, which also broke the old world record. Dennis Mitchell finished in 9.91 seconds. Linford Christie of Great Britain set a European mark with his time of 9.92—and didn't even get a medal! This competition was hailed as the greatest foot race of all time.

A Career Disappointment

The long-jump competition turned out to be every bit the equal of the 100-meter race. Carl had been chasing the Bob Beamon record for a decade. Now he gave the finest performance of his career. Three times, Carl jumped 29 feet or better. He actually outjumped Beamon by going 29 feet 2 3/4 inches, but because of a strong wind, the jump didn't count as an official record. Two leaps later, as the wind fell within legal limits, Carl jumped 29 feet 1 1/4 inch. The Beamon record was so close now that Carl could hardly wait for his next jump.

But as magnificent as Carl was, Mike Powell was even better. On his fifth jump, Mike raced down the runway, exploded off the board, and traveled a distance of 29 feet 4 1/2 inches. After 23 years, Bob Beamon's record had finally been broken, not by Carl Lewis, but by Mike Powell, a 27-year-old Californian.

This was perhaps the most stinging disappointment of Carl's long career. And yet, when he thought about the Tokyo world championships, how could Carl not take pride in his accomplishments?

Slowing Down?

Despite Carl's sensational performance in Tokyo, many people continued to insist that the years were catching up with him. Five weeks before the 1992 Olympics were to begin in Barcelona, Carl ran in a shocking 100-meter final at the Olympic trials in New Orleans, Louisiana, and finished in sixth place. In the 200-meter final, surprisingly, he placed fourth. Only the top three competitors in an event qualify for the Olympic Games. That meant that the best sprinter in history wouldn't be on the Barcelona track. He wouldn't even be a member of the U.S. relay team, which consists of the top four sprinters in the 100 meters. Carl easily made the U.S. team as a long jumper—so did Powell—but that did little to lessen the impact of his failures in the sprints.

All week in New Orleans, Carl kept saying that he didn't feel right. He didn't

Olympic Gold!

know why. He was just missing that extra boost of energy. Although his doctor later announced that Carl had been suffering from a virus, the widespread feeling was that Carl's bigger problem was his age and that the end was possibly drawing near for the 31-year-old champion.

At the Olympic trials in 1992, Carl shocked everyone when he failed to qualify for the 100-meter and 200-meter events.

When he got to Barcelona, Carl joked that he didn't know what he would do with all his free time. He was used to being the busiest man in track and field—competing at the two sprints, the relay and the long jump. It was going to be strange having nothing to worry about but jumping. And it was going to be equally strange not being the constant center of attention.

If there was anything positive about this new position, it was that all of Carl's energies were focused in one direction. The more he heard about how people were writing him off, the more he challenged himself to prove them wrong. It's easy to be confident and successful when things are going well. What sets champions apart, Carl told himself, is how hard you work and how determined you are when you face adversity. As Carl's mother, Evelyn Lewis, has put it, "Carl's a hard-nosed competitor. The bigger the challenge, the better a champion he can be.

What sets champions apart, Carl told himself, is how hard you work ... when you face adversity.

New World Records in Barcelona

As expected, the Olympic long jump came down to the two greats—Carl Lewis and Mike Powell. On the first of his six leaps, Carl traveled 28 feet, 5 1/2 inches. It was a terrific opening effort.

Olympic Gold!

Jumper after jumper vaulted into the pit, but nobody was coming close to that first jump, not even Carl. Mike Powell was struggling with his form. Finally, on his last jump, Mike, who was just getting over a leg injury, hit the board just right and vaulted forward. Sand sprayed when he landed. A huge roar went up from the crowd. Everybody knew it was a superb jump. But was it better than 28 feet 5 1/2 inches?

The measurements were made. They were checked carefully. Carl sat nervously nearby. All he could do was wait and watch—and hope that his rival had not surpassed him. At last, the distance was posted. Mike Powell had jumped 28 feet 4 1/4 inches. It was good for a silver medal, but not good enough to beat Carl, the gold medalist yet again. Carl was now the only man in history to capture three straight Olympic golds in the event.

"He has set the level of excellence for a long time," Mike Powell said afterward.

It turned out that Carl's Olympics didn't begin and end with the long jump, after all. During a preliminary round of the 4 x 100 relay, American sprinter Mark Witherspoon suffered a severely pulled tendon in the back of his foot. Coach Mel Rosen needed a replacement. The coach turned to Carl, who had mixed feelings. He was very sad for his friend Mark, but he was delighted to have a chance to run.

Carl joined a relay team with Mike Marsh, Leroy Burrell, and Dennis Mitchell. He was chosen to run the anchor leg, evidence that he had fully recovered from the health problems he had in the trials.

In his legendary career, Carl Lewis may never have run faster than he did on that Barcelona night of the 4 x 100 relay. When Dennis Mitchell handed him the baton, Carl grasped it cleanly and was instantly at full throttle. He sensed it himself. "Yes! Yes," he yelled, even as his body was screaming down the track. When he blazed across the finish line, the Olympic scoreboard flashed the number: 37.40. *RECORD DEL MUNDO* was the message on the board. Neither Carl nor his relay teammates needed to have any translation. *RECORD DEL MUNDO* is Spanish for *WORLD RECORD*.

Carl leaped into the air once, twice, three times. He leaned back and hurled the baton high into the stands. Someone clocked Carl's 100 meters at 8.8 seconds, which is surely faster than anybody has ever officially run. The stadium erupted in a deafening salute to the four American sprinters. In the Olympics, when he was supposed to be just a supporting actor, Carl was once again the star.

Olympic Gold!

Those who doubted him never stopped him, and neither could anything else.

Carl said he would love to continue competing, right up through the 1996 Games in Atlanta, Georgia. Whatever happens, his standing at the top of the track world will not change. Carl Lewis has won eight gold medals over three Olympics. Five times he has anchored world-record 4 x 100 relays. He has jumped farther than 28 feet more than 60 times. Nobody else even comes close to these achievements.

Carl has accomplished his many feats not only with talent, but with extraordinary drive and determination. Nobody took him seriously when he first started competing as a frail-looking kid in New Jersey and nobody figured he would do too much in Barcelona, either. Those who doubted him never stopped him, and neither could anything else. Just as Carl grew up idolizing the great Jesse Owens, a new generation of American youngsters now dream of being like Carl Lewis. Things had turned out just fine for the runt of the Lewis family. As the Barcelona Games drew to a close, Mike Powell couldn't help but express his great admiration for Carl Lewis. "No doubt about it," Mike Powell said. "He's the best track-and-field athlete ever."

Glossary

blocks Foot supports for a crouching runner right before the start of a race.
false start A foul that is called when a runner leaves the blocks too early.
field events Events that involve jumping and throwing.
foul In jumping, what occurs when a jumper's food edges beyond the takeoff board.
handoff The exchange of the baton between runners in a relay.
heat A preliminary qualifying race.
hitch kick A pedaling motion of the arms and legs that can squeeze extra distance out of a jump.
meter The basic unit of length in the metric system; equals 39.37 inches, or 3.28 feet.
rival One who competes against another.
sprinter One who runs a short distance at a great speed.
steroids Dangerous and illegal drugs that artificially increase an athlete's strength.

For Further Reading

Aaseng, Nathan. *Carl Lewis: Legend Chaser.* Minneapolis: Lerner Publications, 1985.
Arnold, Caroline. *The Olympic Summer Games.* New York: Franklin Watts, 1991.
Duden, Jane. *The Olympics.* New York: Crestwood House, 1991.
Jarrett, William. *Timetables of Sports History: The Olympic Games.* New York: Facts On File, Inc., 1990.
Merrison, Tim. *Field Athletics.* New York: Crestwood House, 1991.
Sandelson, Robert. *Track Athletics.* New York: Crestwood House, 1991.
Tatlow, Peter. *The Olympics.* New York: Franklin Watts, 1988.

Index

B
Beamon, Bob, 11, 12, 17, 18, 25, 26, 56
Brown, Ron, 23, 27
Burrell, Leroy, 55, 56, 61

C
Christie, Linford, 56

D
DeLoach, Joe, 52, 55
Douglas, Joe (agent), 20

G
Graddy, Sam, 23, 24, 27

H
Hemphill, Gina, 28
Hines, Jim, 15

J
Jesse Owens Youth Program, 9
Johnson, Ben, 29, 30–32, 49–52, 55

L
Lattany, Mel, 22
Lewis, Bill (father), 5, 6, 8
    death of, 50, 53
Lewis Carl
    born, 6
    childhood, 5–6, 8–9
    competitions, 10, 11, 12, 15, 17, 18–19, 21, 22, 23–28, 30, 49, 52, 54, 55–56, 59
    hitch kick, 14, 16
    medals, 19, 21, 23, 24, 50, 51, 52, 53, 60, 62
    musical interests, 8
    records, 19, 21, 27, 50, 60, 61
    Sullivan Award, 18
    at University of Houston, 12, 14
    at Willingboro high school, 9–11, 12

Lewis, Carol (sister), 8, 9
Lewis, Cleve (brother), 7, 8
Lewis Evelyn (mother), 6–8, 53, 59
Lewis, Mack (brother), 7

M
Marsh, Mike, 61
Memphis Rogues, 8
Mitchell, Dennis, 55, 56, 61
Moses, Edwin, 21
Myricks, Larry, 17, 21, 24, 50

O
Olympic Games
    in Barcelona, Spain (1992), 57, 59–61
    in Berlin, Germany (1936), 6, 28
    in Los Angeles, United States (1984), 19, 22–28
    in Mexico City, Mexico (1968), 11
    in Moscow, USSR (1980), 6
    in Seoul, South Korea (1988), 30, 32, 49–53
Owens, Jesse, 6, 9, 11, 12, 15, 28, 62

P
Pan American Games, 7
Powell, Mike, 50, 54, 56–57, 59, 60, 62

R
Rosen, Mel (coach), 60

S
Smith, Calvin, 22, 27

T
Tellez, Tom (coach), 12, 13, 14, 15
Tuskegee Institute, 6

W
Witherspoon, Mark, 60

11049

Locust Grove Elementary
31230 Constitution Hwy
Locust Grove, VA 22508